"How – how did that happen?" Lizzie said. "It couldn't have fallen all by itself. How did—"

"I'll give you three guesses," Jessica said curtly.

And then she heard a moan from Lizzie as the air started to shimmer in front of them like a mirage, and the outline of a human form began to appear. Slowly but surely the form became more distinct, the trembling shape grew more solid, and she could make out pale arms, legs that were covered in something navy-blue and two sharp glittering eyes behind a pair of spectacles.

"Oh no," Lizzie groaned. "We were right. It *is* you."

Chapter 1

It was on the day that Jessica came home from school and fell flat on her face on the kitchen floor that she first realized that something strange was going on.

It all happened so quickly – one minute she was carrying a carton of juice from the fridge to the table, the next she was stretched out on the blue vinyl tiles, staring at a growing puddle of spilt orange drink.

Jessica lay there for a moment or two, wondering what had happened. She felt sure that someone had tripped her up, because she distinctly remembered a hand grabbing her ankle just before she fell. But that was impossible. There wasn't anyone else in the kitchen. She lifted her head and peered round, just to make sure. But no one was there. No one at all.

She got to her feet and crossed to the sink to get a cloth to mop up the juice. And then, just as she turned round with the damp cloth in her hand, one of the kitchen chairs rose slowly into the air.

Jessica gaped at the chair in horror. It couldn't be true. Surely she was imagining it? Perhaps she'd bumped her head when she fell. Yes, that was it. She'd hit her head on the floor and now she had concussion and was seeing things. It was the only explanation. Deep down, though, Jessica knew that she *wasn't* dreaming. Someone or something *had* tripped her up. And she knew exactly who it was.

It was a ghost. And not just any ordinary ghost either. It was the ghost of a twelve-year-old girl called Beryl.

Jessica watched as the chair sank back to the floor again. Apart from the pool of orange juice on the floor, the room was back to normal. She crouched down to mop up the juice, hoping that she was wrong, hoping that it wasn't Beryl after all. Perhaps there was a perfectly natural explanation. A small earthquake would have thrown her off balance and sent a chair flying through the air. But Jessica knew that it hadn't been an earthquake. She knew that Beryl was up to her old tricks again.

The faint sound of the front room television told her that her sister Lizzie was at home. Jessica wondered if she'd noticed anything unusual too. She'd go in and ask her.

She rinsed the cloth in the sink and then turned towards the door. There was a bulletin board hanging on the wall and she glanced at it idly as she passed. Then she stopped dead. There was a note on the board that she hadn't seen before, pinned up among the old postcards and dentist's appointment reminders.

She looked at the note for a moment or two, trying to work out what it said. This wasn't easy because the paper was creased and the writing was scratchy and uneven. But it didn't take her long to see that it read:

Don't say I didn't warn you.
This is only the beginning
This House is Haunted, too!

Jessica stared at it and groaned to herself. So she was right. It *was* Beryl. It was starting all over again, just as it had last summer when they were on holiday in Cornwall and first met the ghost.

She snatched the note from the board, sending the drawing pin skittering across the floor. She bent down to pick it up and then, as she stood up again, she was aware of a sudden movement behind her, as though someone was looking over her shoulder. She whirled round but the room was empty.

The kitchen seemed suddenly colder now and Jessica shivered. Then she straightened her shoulders and shouted, "Beryl!"

There was silence.

4

"Beryl!" Jessica shouted again. "I know you're there! You can't frighten me, you know!"

But there was no answer. Jessica shrugged, and went to talk to her sister.

Lizzie was slumped on the sofa, gazing glumly at the television. On the screen, a lot of yelling children were throwing buckets of slimy green liquid at each other.

Jessica paused for a moment to watch and then said, "What's going on?"

"It's a quiz show," Lizzie said. "If you get the answers right then you get green gunk thrown at you."

"That doesn't seem fair," Jessica said. She paused and then went on, "I don't suppose you've noticed anything funny going on, have you?"

Lizzie frowned at her. "Funny? What sort of funny?"

Jessica shrugged. "Oh, odd noises and chairs flying round the room and notes on the board. That kind of thing."

"Notes? What sort of notes?" asked Lizzie,

puzzled. "I don't know what you're going on about."

"*This* sort of note," said Jessica, handing her the crumpled piece of paper.

Lizzie read the message and then looked at Jessica with eyes wide with alarm. "Oh no," she said. "Not Beryl? Tell me it's not Beryl."

"It's Beryl all right," said Jessica. "She's up to her old tricks again."

Lizzie didn't say anything. On the television, the children had stopped throwing green gunk at each other and were pelting each other with tennis balls instead. And then, as they watched, the picture suddenly changed to a lot of middle-aged men in grey suits and glasses shouting at each other.

"Hey, what's going on?" Lizzie said indignantly. "Where's my programme? Who are all those men?"

"It's the House of Commons," Jessica said. "You must have flipped over to another channel."

"But I didn't," said Lizzie. "The remote control's on top of the set. I didn't touch it."

"Well, it can't have changed all by itself."

"It must have done. Look, it's switched over to Channel Four now. What's going on?"

"I'll give you three guesses," Jessica said grimly.

The girls stared open-mouthed as one channel after another flashed on to the set. Then Jessica reached for the remote control and switched it off.

"I think that our friend Beryl's discovered the magic of modern technology," she said.

"Oh, that explains it," Lizzie said. "I found my *Space Rats* computer game playing all by itself the other day. But I thought you'd been fiddling with it. And now I come to think of it, other odd things *have* been happening. There was that morning when everyone's shoes disappeared and we found them all piled up in the middle of the kitchen floor."

"Yes, *I* got the blame for that," Jessica said darkly. "As if I'd do anything so stupid."

"So it was Beryl all the time?" Lizzie said.

"Who else could it have been?" Jessica asked. "It wasn't me and it couldn't have been

Mum or Andrew."

"I'm not so sure about that," Jessica said. "Andrew often plays practical jokes."

Andrew was their stepfather and he had a good sense of humour. Most of the time.

"But he'd never do anything as childish as taking our shoes," Lizzie said. "And even if he did, he'd own up right away. He wouldn't let you take the blame."

"And now there's this note on the board," Jessica went on. She had decided not to say anything about being tripped up.

"So we're being haunted again," Lizzie said.

"That's what it looks like."

"Perhaps we're mistaken," Lizzie said hopefully. "Perhaps it isn't really—"

"No, I don't think we're mistaken," Jessica said. "It really does look as though this house is haunted too!"

Chapter 2

"I don't believe it," Lizzie said faintly. "It can't be happening all over again. Not here. It *can't*."

"We'd better be prepared for the worst," Jessica said.

"Tell me I'm just imagining this," Lizzie moaned. "It was bad enough the last time. Don't you remember?"

Jessica nodded. How could she ever forget? They had rented a cottage in Cornwall for their summer holiday that year, in a little seaside village called Ottercombe. It had been their first holiday together as a new family – she and Lizzie and their mother, along with

Andrew and his two sons from his first marriage, Martin and Gareth. Everything had been fine at first, until the day that Jessica had found a note pinned to the notice board in the cottage, a note that read:

Beware! This House is Haunted!

They'd all thought then that someone was playing tricks until strange things started to happen – noises and screams in the night, and crockery breaking, and people being pushed downstairs. And then Beryl had appeared. She was the ghost of a twelve-year-old schoolgirl who'd been knocked off her bike and killed in 1934 and who'd been haunting the cottage ever since.

Jessica and Lizzie and the boys had become friends with Beryl for a while. But that all changed when Beryl turned out to be un-friendly and spiteful and her hauntings became even more noisy and dangerous. Their perfect holiday soon turned into a nightmare. The grown-ups hadn't realized what was happening, of course, and blamed the children for all the noise and damage. The unfairness of this was even worse than the chaos caused by the ghost. In the end, though, when Beryl's hauntings had become too much to take, they had cut the holiday short and come home.

And that had seemed to be the end of the story. The last of Beryl. Until now.

"I *knew* this was going to happen," Jessica said. "The minute I saw the cat."

"The cat?" Lizzie asked.

"Yes, don't you remember? The black china cat from the cottage. That's how she got here."

"Yes, of course," said Lizzie. "You're right. It's the only way she could have done it."

The girls had learned from Beryl that a ghost can leave a house it is haunting if something that belongs to the house is taken away. The ghost can then travel with it, if it wants to. They'd been able to take Beryl to the beach with them by hiding a small black china cat from the cottage in the bag with their swimming things. And it was this same china cat that they had found in their luggage when they arrived back from Cornwall at the end of the holiday.

"What I'd really like to know is how that cat got into our luggage in the first place," Jessica said grimly. "I certainly didn't put it there."

"Perhaps Beryl hid it there herself," Lizzie suggested.

"I've just remembered something," Jessica said. "When we came back from Cornwall I found a note on the board in the kitchen."

"What did it say?" Lizzie asked.

"*Beware! This house is haunted too!*" Jessica said. "I didn't think anything of it at the time. I couldn't believe that Beryl had really come back with us. So I threw it away and forgot all about it. But she must have been here all the time. Ever since we came back."

"But why hasn't she done anything till now?" Lizzie asked. "Why has she been so quiet?"

Jessica shrugged. "Dunno. Perhaps she's had other things to think about."

"Where's the cat now?" Lizzie asked.

"I'm not sure," said Jessica. "I think I put it in a drawer somewhere. Mum said I had to post it back to the owner of the cottage. What was her name again?"

"Mrs Pengelly," Lizzie said.

"Yes, that's right. I was supposed to post it back to Mrs Pengelly with a letter of apology but I forgot all about it. Until now."

"So Beryl's been here all the time and we didn't even know it." Lizzie looked nervously round the room, and shivered. "We've got to think very carefully before we do anything. We don't want to be stuck with her for ever."

Jessica looked at her sister's nervous face and smiled. "Don't worry," she said. "If Beryl *is* here, we'll soon get the better of her. We're on home ground, remember. We've got the advantage this time."

"I'm not so sure," Lizzie said. "Do you remember what Beryl said when we last saw her?"

Jessica cast her mind back to Beryl's final appearance in the cottage in Cornwall. She remembered the sharp black eyes glittering behind the round glasses; she remembered the stained and creased gym-slip, the wrinkled blue woollen stockings, the straight hair cut in a short untidy bob. How could anyone be afraid of a ghost that looked like an old-fashioned schoolgirl?

"Can you remember what she said?" Lizzie repeated.

"No, not exactly. Can you?"

"Oh yes," said Lizzie. "I can remember every word. She said: *Don't think you've seen the last of me yet. Because you haven't. You haven't seen the last of me.*"

Jessica shivered. The room suddenly seemed very cold, as though someone had opened a door somewhere and let in a draught. But the front room door was firmly closed.

And then there was the sudden sound of something breaking and both girls jumped and turned round. A small vase had fallen from the windowsill and was lying on the carpet, broken into several pieces.

"How – how did that happen?" Lizzie said.

"It couldn't have fallen all by itself. How did—"

"I'll give you three guesses," Jessica said curtly.

And then she heard a moan from Lizzie as the air started to shimmer in front of them like a mirage, and the outline of a human form began to appear. Slowly but surely the form became more distinct, the trembling shape grew more solid, and she could make out pale arms, legs that were covered in something navy-blue and two sharp glittering eyes behind a pair of spectacles.

"Oh no," Lizzie groaned. "We were right. It *is* you."

"Yes," said Beryl, her thin mouth twisted into a sneer. "That's right. It's me. You could at least be a bit more welcoming."

Lizzie didn't know what to say. She stared at Beryl and the ghost grinned back, her eyes full of malice.

"So you've been here all this time," Jessica said. "You've kept very quiet about it."

Beryl flopped down in an armchair. "Well,

there's been so much to do," she said. "You've got all sorts of topping things here. Your television's super. Much nicer than the one in the cottage. And I love that machine underneath it for recording things when you aren't there."

"The video recorder," Jessica said.

"Yes, that's it. And the kitchen's wizard. Especially that sweet little box that cooks things so quickly. The micro-something or other."

"I suppose it was you who was messing about with my computer," Lizzie said severely.

"Oh yes, I've had great fun with that too," Beryl said. "So, what with one thing and another, I haven't really had much time for ordinary haunting."

"So what's made you start again now?" Jessica asked. "I assume it *was* you who tripped me up in the kitchen just now."

Lizzie stared at Jessica. "You didn't tell me about—" she began but was interrupted by a cackle of laughter from Beryl.

"Yes, that was me, all right," she said. "If only you could have seen yourself! What a hoot!"

"So why are you bothering with us now?" Jessica asked.

"I'm getting rather bored with all those machines," Beryl said languidly. "People are so much more fun. And I'm tired of this silly house of yours. The cottage in Cornwall was far nicer."

"Don't tell me you're feeling homesick!" Jessica sneered.

"And what's wrong with that?" Beryl demanded. "I've got feelings too, you know. It's not much fun being knocked off your bicycle when you're only twelve and then having to spend the next umpteen years haunting beastly people like you."

"If you're looking for sympathy, forget it," Jessica snapped. "You're not welcome here and the sooner you get out the better."

Beryl gave her an icy stare. "You needn't think you're going to get rid of me as easily as that," she said. "You'll have to try very much

harder. And anyway, the fun is only just beginning. I'm going to make your lives very
uncomfortable from now on. Very uncomfortable indeed."

"We're not frightened of you," Jessica said
defiantly. "You didn't get the better of us last
time. And you won't get the better of us
now."

"Oh, won't I?" said Beryl. "We'll soon see
about that. Oh yes, we'll soon see about that."

Then, as they watched in amazement, she
began to fade and dissolve, until her body had
become a shimmering shape that drifted in the
air like smoke, before vanishing completely.

Chapter 3

It took Jessica a long time to get to sleep that night. Every time she began to feel drowsy, she would remember Beryl's grinning face and feel wide awake again. She felt sure that the ghost must be planning something and that any minute now the air would be filled with ghastly shrieks and other hideous noises. She thought about Beryl's hauntings in the cottage in Cornwall, remembering the awful screaming and the overturned furniture, and how frightened they had been at first. She dreaded to think what would happen if Beryl got up to her old tricks in this house. It seemed such an unlikely place for a ghost to haunt, anyway. The holiday cottage had at least been old and full of character. But this neat modern house with its patio and tidy lawns was the very last place you would expect to find a ghost.

There was a sudden sharp noise and Jessica sat up in bed, her heart pounding. But it was only a car door slamming in the road outside, and she sank back on the pillow again.

She must have drifted off to sleep then, because some time afterwards she woke up with a start. She had a feeling that a noise had disturbed her but she couldn't be sure. She stared into the darkness, listening, knowing that something was wrong. But the house was silent, and all she could hear was the sound of her own breathing. Oh well, perhaps she'd only imagined it. Perhaps she was just expecting the worst because she was scared what Beryl might do next, and because she remembered the sort of things that Beryl had done in the past. She lay back and closed her eyes but her heart was pounding and she felt too wide awake to sleep.

And then she heard it. A low moaning noise. It seemed to be coming from the foot of her bed. Then, as Jessica sat up, the moaning rose to a high-pitched whine.

"Oh, do keep quiet, Beryl!" Jessica shouted. "We're not impressed, you know. It'll take more than that to frighten me!"

The noise stopped abruptly, almost as if the ghost had heard what she said and was thinking about it. Then Jessica heard a familiar mocking voice in her ear. "Don't worry," said Beryl. "I can do much better than that. You *know* I can. I'm only just warming up. Getting into my stride." She gave a harsh metallic laugh. "Just you wait and see."

Jessica shut her eyes and groaned. She knew exactly what was going to happen next. Sure enough, the moaning started again and swiftly rose to a high-pitched shriek. It was soon followed by hideous cackles of laughter, and by violent bumps and thuds that sounded as though someone was throwing furniture about in the hallway.

Jessica pulled the duvet over her head and

tried to pretend that nothing was happening. If she ignored the noise then perhaps Beryl would get bored and stop. But, as the screams grew even more shrill and the banging even louder, she realized that Beryl wasn't going to give up so easily.

At last she could stand it no longer and got out of bed. She opened the bedroom door and shouted, "Shut up, Beryl! No one's impressed, you know. So keep *quiet*!"

It was only then that Jessica realized that the landing light was on and that her mother was standing there in her dressing gown, staring at her. Lizzie was standing sleepily beside her. And it was then that she noticed too that the noises had suddenly stopped and there was no sound at all.

"Now then, Jessica, what exactly is going on?" her mother asked in a voice that could shatter glass. "And who *exactly* is Beryl?"

Chapter 4

Jessica was late down for breakfast the next morning. This was partly because she had overslept but mainly because she couldn't bear to face the others after what had happened the night before. If she put off going downstairs, with any luck they would all have finished breakfast before she appeared.

But her luck was out. When she walked into the kitchen, they were still at the table, munching toast and marmalade. She sat down without looking at anyone and there was silence for a moment or two. Then Andrew said jovially, "Well, I'm glad you could make it at last, Jess."

Jessica shot him a murderous look and then helped herself to a generous portion of Ricey-Pops.

"You could at least say good morning," her mother said. "It's the least you could do after disturbing us all with that noise last night."

"It wasn't me," Jessica mumbled, reaching for the milk.

"The sounds were coming from your room," her mother said acidly. "If it wasn't you, then who was it?"

"I don't know," Jessica said. "I just don't know."

"I'm afraid I don't believe you," her mother went on. "I must say that I'm really disappointed, Jessica. I thought we had seen the last of these displays of bad behaviour when we left Cornwall. But it seems that you intend to carry on with them here. Well, I'm telling you plainly that it has got to stop. Do you hear me? It must stop at once." She paused to take a sip of coffee and then went on, "Your Aunt Thelma is coming for lunch today. The last thing we want is a display of this kind while *she's* here."

Jessica groaned to herself. She hated Aunt Thelma. She was her mother's elder sister and a real pain in the neck. It was bad enough having to cope with a ghost in the house without having to face an awful aunt as well. On balance, she thought she'd rather have the ghost than the aunt. At least Beryl was unpredictable. You never knew what was going to happen next. But with Aunt Thelma you knew *exactly* what was going to happen next. All she ever did was talk without stopping. Mainly about herself.

"I don't see why we have to be there," Jessica said grumpily. "Can't you have lunch without us?"

"Of course you've got to be there," her mother said firmly. "Your Aunt Thelma's very fond of you."

"Well, she's got a funny way of showing it," said Jessica. "She never gets my name right. And whenever she asks a question she never bothers to listen to the answer but carries on saying something else."

"I've just remembered something," Lizzie

said brightly. "Mandy Hopkins asked me to go round to her house this lunchtime to listen to a new CD she got for her birthday."

"No, she didn't," her mother said briskly. "Now I've had quite enough of this. You are both going to be here when Thelma arrives and you are both going to be polite and well behaved. Understood?"

There was silence, broken only by the sound of toast being munched. Then Andrew said, "Jess, I don't suppose you're responsible for that silly note on the board, by any chance?"

Jessica gaped at him. "What do you mean?" she asked. "What silly note?"

"There's a note on the board," Andrew said. "Like the ones we used to find on the board at the cottage in Cornwall."

Jessica got up from her seat and crossed to the board, aware that three pairs of eyes were boring into her back as she went. Andrew was right. The note was there all right. It read:

That was just the Beginning.

Don't say I didn't warn you.
Signed Beryl Bowditch (Miss)

Jessica pulled the note from the board and tore it into small pieces. "Just someone playing the fool," she mumbled as she returned to the table.

"Well, all I hope is that we've seen the last of this bad behaviour," her mother said icily. "Because if not…" She left the sentence unfinished and gave them all a meaningful look. Then she got up from her chair and said, "As Jessica was the last one down, she can do the washing-up."

"That's not fair!" Jessica protested.

"Neither is being woken in the night by screams and banging," her mother snapped. "So just do as you're told." She turned and walked out of the kitchen.

Andrew watched her go and then turned to the others. "She's right, you know. You've got to stop all this messing about. It's getting beyond a joke." He gave them a weary smile and then followed Jessica's mother out of the room.

As soon as the door closed behind them, Lizzie said, "I suppose that was Beryl up to her old tricks last night?"

Jessica nodded. "I just can't believe that we're still stuck with her," she said grimly. "And it's worse now because she's in *our* house this time and not the other way round."

There was a pause, and then Lizzie said, "Well, there's nothing else for it. We'll just have to ask her to behave herself."

Jessica gave a scornful laugh. "You must be joking!"

Lizzie took no notice. "We can tell her that we don't mind her being here as long as she doesn't do anything to annoy people."

"Is that the best you can come up with?" Jessica said.

"Can you think of anything better?" Lizzie asked.

Jessica gave her a nasty look and then raised her head and shouted, "Beryl! We want to talk to you! We know you're there! Somewhere!"

There was a silence as they waited for something to happen.

"She's not coming," Lizzie said at last. "Perhaps we should put a note on the board."

Jessica gave her an impatient glance and then shouted again, "Beryl! We're waiting for you!"

Lizzie was the first to notice the shimmering shape hanging in the air. Then they both watched spellbound as the vague outline became clearer until, before long, the familiar figure of Beryl was standing in front of them, her eyes glittering and her mouth twisted in the sneer that they knew so well.

Jessica stared at her for a moment. She looked so out of place in their clean, modern kitchen, this twelve-year-old ghost in an old-fashioned school uniform.

"What is it this time?" Beryl said impatiently.

"We just — we just wanted to say that we'd like you to go away as soon as possible, please," Lizzie said.

Beryl gave a sharp laugh that sounded like a bark. "And what if I don't want to go?" she said. "It's chilly in that cottage at this time of year. It may be boring here but at least it's warm. No, I think I'll stay."

There was a pause, and then Lizzie said, "How exactly did you get here in the first place? Did *you* hide that cat in our luggage?"

Beryl gave her a scornful look. "No, it wasn't me. It was one of those boys you were on holiday with. The one with the glasses."

"I knew it!" Jessica said furiously. "Just wait till I get my hands on that little—"

"Do you mean that Gareth hid the cat?" Lizzie asked in amazement. "*Gareth?*"

During their holiday together in Cornwall, Gareth had always seemed the more timid of Andrew's two sons. It was hard to imagine him doing anything as adventurous as helping to smuggle a ghost back to London.

"Of course it was my idea really," Beryl said. "He didn't want to do it at first. But I soon persuaded him that it would be a jolly good wheeze and so he hid the cat in your bag."

"But why?" Jessica asked. "Why did you want to leave the cottage anyway?"

"I thought it would make a nice change to come home with you. And it would also serve you jolly well right for being so horrid to me before you went away."

"You deserved it," Lizzie muttered.

"What do you mean?"

Beryl's eyes had begun to glitter dangerously and Jessica said quickly, "Well, now that you're here you must promise to behave yourself from now on. You must promise not to make a nuisance of yourself any more."

"And what if I don't?" said Beryl.

Jessica gaped at her. "Well, if you don't, we – er – we won't be friends with you," she muttered at last, knowing how feeble she sounded.

"Oh dear," said Beryl, pretending to be dismayed. "How simply awful! Pardon me while I have a good cry." She gave a couple of loud theatrical sniffs and then moved closer to Jessica. The ghost's eyes were like two black stones and Jessica backed nervously away. "So," Beryl hissed, "if I don't promise to be good, you won't be friends with me? Well, let me tell you a little secret. Just between the three of us. Believe it or not, I don't *want* to be friends with you. I don't even like you. And I'm going to stay here for as long as I want. And that may well be for ever!" She laughed out loud then and, as she did so, began to fade before their eyes. In a moment she was gone.

It was Lizzie who broke the silence at last. "Well, you didn't handle that very well, did you?" she sneered. "It doesn't look as though we're ever going to get rid of Beryl now."

Jessica glared at her. "I'll think of something," she said. "Just you wait and see."

She hoped that she sounded more confident than she felt. But she had a very nasty feeling that Lizzie was right.

Chapter 5

"Ah, there you are, Jennifer," said Aunt Thelma. "We were wondering what had happened to you. Weren't we, Keith?"

Jessica had put off seeing Aunt Thelma for as long as she could. When she and Uncle Keith had drawn up outside the house in their Volvo, Jessica had gone straight upstairs to her room. If anyone asked her what she was doing, she was going to tell them that she was working on a school project. Fortunately no one noticed her absence, so she was spared having to tell a lie. But when lunchtime came, there was nothing else for it – she had to join the others and be polite to Aunt Thelma.

"Hello," Jessica muttered as she sat down. Uncle Keith smiled at her and nodded, but Aunt Thelma carried on talking about the new curtains she was planning for her lounge. She was plump and blonde and wearing rather too much make-up as usual. It was hard to believe that she and Jessica's mother were sisters.

"So you went to Cornwall for your holidays this year, did you?" Aunt Thelma said, gazing suspiciously at her plate.

"Yes," said Jessica's mother. "We had a lovely—"

"It's years since *we* went to Cornwall," Aunt Thelma went on, taking no notice. "We used to go there quite a bit when we were younger but we like warmer places now, don't we, Keith? You ought to try Majorca or Ibiza next time. They're a bit crowded, of course, but I don't expect *you'll* mind that. Of course we went to Florida in the spring, but not everyone can afford it, can they?" She paused to take a mouthful of cottage pie. "We're thinking of another cruise next year. To

Greece and Turkey and places like that. Or the Caribbean perhaps. Keith isn't too sure, though, are you, dear?"

Uncle Keith opened his mouth to say something but Aunt Thelma wasn't interested. "We do find that a nicer class of people go on cruises. More *select*, if you know what I mean." She turned to Jessica again. "Did you have a nice time in Cornwall, Gillian dear?" Jessica wisely ignored her and concentrated on her own helping of cottage pie.

"I've never really cared for Italy, though," Aunt Thelma was saying now. "Too many old churches, if you ask me. After all, when you've seen one old church you've seen them all, haven't you? Of course, Keith likes all those works of art in Italy but I can take them or leave them. I always say there's nothing quite like a nice beach. Don't you agree, Gemma?"

There was a sudden pause and Jessica realized with a start that everyone was looking at her. She was obviously expected to say something.

"Oh yes," she said, "there's nothing quite like a nice beach. In Cornwall—"

But Aunt Thelma wasn't listening. She was rattling on about a lovely couple from Macclesfield they'd met on their last visit to Tenerife.

Jessica carried on with her cottage pie and tried to pretend she was somewhere else. She could tell from their glazed expressions that the others were doing the same thing. Her mother was the only one who was even pretending to be interested.

"I see what you mean about your aunt being an awful old bat."

For a moment Jessica thought that Aunt Thelma was talking to her again. And then she gasped when she realized that what she could hear was Beryl's voice whispering in her ear. She turned round but there was no sign of her. Perhaps she'd just imagined it.

"What a boring old windbag!"

Yes, it was definitely Beryl. There was no mistaking that familiar metallic voice. Jessica looked wildly round at the others, scared that they too could hear what Beryl was saying. But she needn't have worried – Aunt Thelma's shrill voice was drowning out all other sounds.

"I don't know how you can stand it," Beryl whispered. "She's driving *me* mad, and I don't have to sit around and listen to the old cow."

"Oh, why don't you just shut up!" Jessica said loudly.

There was a sudden shocked silence. Jessica realized with a start that Aunt Thelma had stopped talking and that everyone was staring at her.

"What's the matter?" she asked, and then realized to her horror that everyone must have heard what she said.

"Yes, well, I – I'm sorry," she stammered, "I was thinking of something else. I mean, I wasn't talking to…" Her voice tailed off and she stared miserably at her plate. She could hardly explain that she had only been talking to a ghost called Beryl.

"Yes, well, I can see that your manners haven't improved since I last saw you," Aunt

Thelma said briskly. "It's high time you learned a few social graces, Janice." She turned back to Jessica's mother. "Now then, what was I saying? Oh yes, we had a nice time in Egypt too, but I didn't really take to the place somehow. All that sand. And you couldn't get a decent cup of tea for love nor money."

Jessica pushed her plate to one side and glanced at Uncle Keith who was sitting beside her. He gave her a friendly wink and she smiled back.

"Do you want me to get rid of her?" Beryl said in her ear.

"No," Jessica whispered. "Don't do—"

"What was that, Jess?" said her mother. "Did you say something?"

"*No!*" Jessica said, hoping that Beryl would get the message too.

"I thought you said something, that's all." She stood up. "Well, if everyone's finished, I'll fetch in the sweet."

"That was very nice, dear," said Aunt Thelma. "Plain and wholesome. I'm glad you didn't go to any trouble on our behalf."

"Are you sure you don't want me to get rid of her?" said Beryl.

Jessica didn't dare say anything out loud. She shook her head vigorously, and then caught Andrew looking at her with a puzzled expression and tried to pretend that she had a crick in her neck.

Her mother came back to the table with a large bowl of trifle and another of fruit salad. "Now then, Thelma, will you try some trifle?" she said.

"Yes, please," said Aunt Thelma. "I haven't had trifle for years. Our foreign travels have given us a taste for rather more sophisticated fare. Isn't that so, Keith? Mind you, there's nothing wrong with trifle. In its place."

"Oh dear," Jessica's mother said. "I've forgotten the spoons."

She disappeared into the kitchen, closely followed by Andrew who was clearly desperate to get away from Aunt Thelma. "I'll just put the kettle on for coffee," he mumbled as the door closed behind them.

Then the table gave a sudden lurch and

everyone gasped.

"Goodness, what was that?" said Aunt Thelma.

"Perhaps it was an earth tremor," suggested Lizzie.

"In East Finchley? Don't be ridiculous," said Aunt Thelma.

The table lurched again. The bowls and plates rattled, and the water jug wobbled dangerously.

"What's happening?" Aunt Thelma said nervously. "Are your children moving the table?"

"No, of course not," said Jessica, and, at the same time, a voice in her ear said, "But *I* am!"

"No, don't!" she shouted.

Everyone stared at Jessica again and then they forgot that she had said anything at all as a plate suddenly flew off the table and smashed to pieces against the wall, closely followed by another. The table rocked and swayed again, and knives and spoons tumbled on to the carpet.

"Stop it, Beryl, please!" Jessica shouted.

She saw Lizzie's face staring at her in alarm as an unseen hand began to tug at the tablecloth. Jessica seized the cloth with both hands and tried to prevent it being pulled away.

"Whose side are you on?" Beryl hissed in her ear, and then Jessica's chair toppled over and she landed on her back on the floor.

As she got to her feet, she could hear Aunt Thelma making strange yelping noises and someone shouting as the table rocked and swayed and plates and spoons and glasses continued to fall. And then, to her horror, she saw the bowl of trifle rise slowly into the air and empty itself all over Aunt Thelma.

Aunt Thelma screamed and, as she did so, the room fell silent. The table stopped rocking and the crockery stopped falling. Everyone stared in horrified silence at Aunt Thelma and at the thick gooey mixture of jam and custard and cream and jelly slithering over her hair and face and shoulders.

"Well," said Beryl in Jessica's ear. "That soon shut her up, didn't it?"

Chapter 6

"I just don't understand what got into you," their mother said angrily as soon as Aunt Thelma had left.

"It wasn't us," Lizzie said sullenly. "We didn't do it."

"Well, who did then?" Andrew had asked. "You're not trying to tell me that the table rocked by itself? That the plates broke against the wall all on their own? That the trifle emptied itself all over Aunt Thelma?"

"But it *wasn't* us," Lizzie said.

Her mother sighed. "Of course it was, Elizabeth. Who else could it have been?"

Lizzie gulped. Her mother only ever called

her Elizabeth when she was really cross. "I didn't see who did it," she said. "Did you?"

"Well, no, I didn't," her mother snapped. "I was in the kitchen when it happened. And so was Andrew. So it *must* have been one of you children. Now get out of my sight while I clean up. I'll decide what to do with you later. In the meantime you can think of a way to apologize to Aunt Thelma. How I'll ever be able to look her in the face again, I don't know…"

Jessica went into the front room and slumped down on the sofa. Lizzie trailed miserably after her. They stared at the blank television screen for a moment or two and then Lizzie said, "I've never seen Mum as angry as this before."

"Neither have I," said Jessica.

"It's not fair. It wasn't my fault."

"It wasn't my fault either."

Neither of them actually said whose fault it was, but they both knew. It was just that blaming a ghost for all that had happened would have sounded too fantastic for words if spoken out loud. They certainly couldn't have told their mother the truth.

To make things even worse, they now had to apologize to Aunt Thelma. She had gone home as soon as the worst of the trifle had been cleaned from her dress. She hadn't said anything at all to the children before she went but Uncle Keith had smiled at Jessica when he said goodbye and whispered, "I rather enjoyed all that."

But there was no getting away from the fact that their mother was furious. Even Andrew, usually so pleasant and easy-going, was angry and puzzled by what had happened. Life was clearly going to be very difficult for a while.

"We've got to persuade Beryl to behave herself," Jessica said. "We've got to appeal to her better nature."

"She hasn't *got* a better nature," Lizzie said. "Surely you know that. Don't you remember how kind we were to her in Cornwall? Taking her with us to the beach and arranging that party so that she could meet her brother and sisters? And look how she repaid us."

"Well, what else do you suggest?" Jessica wanted to know. "We've got to try."

Lizzie looked round the room and then called out, "Beryl, are you there? We want to talk to you."

There was a pause while they waited for something to happen.

Lizzie tried again. "Beryl!" she shouted. "We want—"

"All right, all right," sounded a familiar voice. "There's no need to shout." And then, suddenly, Beryl was there, a vague shape at first, hanging in the air like a wisp of smoke. And then the smoke thickened, strengthened, became a human shape.

"That was wizard, wasn't it?" Beryl said gleefully, settling down on the sofa next to Lizzie. Lizzie inched nervously away.

"No, it wasn't," Jessica said severely. "We're in real trouble, thanks to you."

"Why did you do it?" Lizzie asked. "Why can't you behave yourself? You know that we get the blame for everything you do."

Beryl looked at her in bewilderment. "But I thought you hated that ghastly woman," she said. "I heard you say so. You said that you couldn't stand her."

"Yes, that's true," Lizzie said. "But we didn't want you to break things. We didn't want you to pour that trifle all over her."

Beryl's expression hardened and she glared defiantly at the girls with her sharp dark eyes. "I was only doing you a favour," she said. "I thought you'd enjoy it. I thought you wanted to get rid of her."

"We *did* want to get rid of her," Jessica said. "And we did rather enjoy it. But *we've* got the blame. Goodness knows what Mum's going to do as a punishment."

"Well, I don't think it's fair," Beryl said. "This is the very last time I do anything to help you. I wanted to be pals with you. I've bent over backwards to be friendly. But that's all over now."

Jessica gaped at her. "Friendly? Waking us up in the middle of the night and throwing things and pushing furniture around and pouring trifle over Aunt Thelma. Is that what you call being friendly?"

"It's what I call having fun," Beryl

snapped. "But things are going to be different from now on. Very different indeed."

Jessica stared at her in alarm and, as she did so, Beryl began to fade before her eyes until all that could be seen of the ghost was a faint shimmering in the air. Then nothing.

And then Jessica almost jumped out of her skin at a sudden blast of sound behind her. She whirled round and saw that the television set had been switched on with the volume turned up as loud as it could go. Lizzie dashed across to switch the set off and, as she did so, there was another eruption of sound from the radio on the other side of the room. And then, the minute she turned the radio off, the television switched itself on again. Jessica ran to the television again and was halfway back to the radio when she realized that the room was silent once more.

She sank down on the sofa and then Beryl's unmistakable voice sounded in her ear. "That was fun, wasn't it?" she hissed. "Now let's see how fast you can move this time."

The television switched itself on again and,

at the same time, the radio came on and then there was another noise too, a strange roaring sound from the direction of the kitchen. Jessica ran to switch off the television and the radio while Lizzie raced into the kitchen where she found that the washing machine had been switched on and that the vacuum cleaner was roaring away in the cupboard under the stairs. It was when the lights started switching themselves on and off that the girls finally gave up and slumped down at the kitchen table, angry and out of breath.

"What on earth is going on?" came a sudden voice, and Jessica looked up to see her mother staring at them from the doorway. "What was all that noise? What do you two think you're doing?"

Jessica realized that all the machines were silent once more, and she grinned with relief.

"I don't think it's at all funny," her mother snapped. "Why on earth were you making all that noise?"

"I don't know," Jessica said weakly. "I mean—"

Her mother sighed. "I did hope that you might have mended your ways after that performance at lunchtime," she said. "But it looks as though I was wrong. If this sort of thing carries on then I'll—"

"But you have to admit that Aunt Thelma looked funny," Lizzie said quickly, "with trifle all over her face."

"No, it's not at all funny, Elizabeth," her mother said severely. "There's nothing at all to laugh at." Then she began to smile, trying hard to keep a straight face at the same time. "Now, I don't want to hear another peep out of either of you." She turned and left the room.

Lizzie looked at Jessica. "What are we going to do?" she whispered.

Jessica shook her head. "I don't know. I just don't know."

"We've got to do *something*," said Lizzie. "Beryl said that things are going to get even worse from now on."

"I know," said Jessica. "That ghost's going to make our lives a misery until we do something about it."

It took Beryl a day or two to get into her stride. Her hauntings were mild and insignificant at first, and the girls began to wonder whether her heart was really in it. Sometimes they would be woken in the night by odd banging noises and wailings in the loft, but Andrew blamed this on the plumbing and arranged for someone to come and inspect it. And there were other minor irritations, too, like the video recorder switching itself on and off for no apparent reason, and plates sliding from the table on to the floor, and pictures suddenly falling from the walls. And then things suddenly started to go missing: library books, for instance, and odd shoes and the key to the garden shed and an entire chicken from the fridge.

After that the hauntings became more spectacular. The banging at night grew too loud to be plumbing and the screams too shrill to be next door's television, and Andrew was tripped on the stairs one morning and nearly broke his neck falling to the bottom.

The girls were blamed, of course, but this

time they didn't bother to argue. They could hardly tell their mother and Andrew that a ghost was responsible. Well, they *could*, but who would believe it?

"Our only hope is that things get so bad that they send us away somewhere," Lizzie said gloomily, after the disturbances had been going on for a week.

"Where?" asked Jessica.

"Oh, I don't know. Anywhere. Boarding school or something. Then they'd *know* it wasn't us. And we'd get away from Beryl."

"Knowing Beryl, she'd find a way of coming with us," Jessica said.

"You're right. I would," came a familiar voice, and the girls looked round to see Beryl leering at them from an armchair. "I hope you're enjoying yourselves," the ghost went on. "I know that I am."

"Why don't you stop it?" said Lizzie. "*Please* stop it. We're in such trouble because of you. It's not fair. We've done nothing to hurt *you*."

"You brought me here," Beryl hissed. "You

brought me to this awful house."

"You can't blame us for that," Lizzie said. "You were the one who got Gareth to hide the cat in our bag. We couldn't have brought you back home with the cat if you hadn't wanted to come here. So it's all *your* fault!"

"Anyway, you've made your point," Jessica said. "You've proved that you're the most brilliant ghost in the world. So why don't you just go away and leave us in peace?"

"All right," said Beryl.

The girls stared at her. "What did you say?" asked Lizzie in surprise.

"I said all right. I'll do it."

"You mean you'll stop the haunting?" asked Jessica.

"Yes." Beryl stared at her with an amused expression on her thin, pale face. "I'll stop the haunting. If you take me home."

"Back to Cornwall?" asked Jessica.

Beryl nodded. "That's right. Take me back to my cottage in Cornwall. That's all you have to do. It couldn't be simpler, could it?"

"But how do we—" Lizzie began.

"The cat, of course," said Jessica. "If we take the cat back to Cornwall, Beryl will go with it." She looked at the ghost. "That's right, isn't it?"

"Yes," Beryl said. "I'm ready to go whenever you are."

"But it isn't as simple as that," Jessica said. "There's a lot to organize."

"Like what, for instance?" Beryl was beginning to sound impatient.

"Like exactly how we're going to get back to Cornwall in the first place," Jessica snapped. "We can't just get into a car and drive there, you know."

There was silence for a moment as they all thought about this. Then Lizzie suddenly let out an excited yelp. "I've got it!"

"Got what?" Jessica asked.

"The answer to the problem, of course." Lizzie's eyes were shining with delight. "It's so simple. *We* don't need to go to Cornwall at all. All we have to do is exactly what Mum said we should do in the first place."

"You mean…?"

"Yes," said Lizzie. "We can send Beryl back by post."

Jessica could tell by the disgusted expression on Beryl's face that she didn't think this was a good idea at all.

"Send me back by *post*?" the ghost said frostily. "By *post*? Like a parcel? Wrapped up with brown paper and string?"

"Well, yes – er – no, not really," Lizzie said nervously. "The cat will be in the parcel, not you. At least, I don't think—"

"We'll wrap the cat very carefully," Jessica said quickly. "We'll use lots of cotton wool and that bubble wrap stuff. It won't get broken."

Beryl was drumming her fingers angrily on the arm of her chair. "You're forgetting one thing," she said.

"What's that?" Lizzie asked. "It all sounds perfectly straightforward to me."

"Well, it would to *you*," Beryl snapped, "but anyone with more than one brain cell would see a basic flaw in your cunning wheeze."

"I think I know what it is," Jessica said wearily.

"Really?" Beryl shot her an icy smile. "And what is that, pray?"

"There's no point in posting the cat back if you won't go with it."

"Exactly!" Beryl said triumphantly. "And I have no intention whatsoever of travelling through His Majesty's mail in a parcel. So there!"

"*Her* Majesty's," Lizzie said absently.

"What?" Beryl snapped.

"*Her* Majesty's mail. We've got a queen now. Queen Elizabeth the Second."

"Really?" said Beryl with interest. "It was King George the Fifth when I died."

"I think he was our queen's grandfather," Lizzie said.

"Can we forget about kings and queens for a moment?" Jessica said irritably. "We've got more important things to think about." She glared at Beryl. "So what you're saying is that you won't go back to Cornwall unless we take you there ourselves?"

"That's right," Beryl said. "I always knew you were brighter than your sister." She gave them a cold smile. "As I was saying, I'm ready to go whenever you are. But don't be too long about it, will you? I don't want to start being beastly again."

She gave the girls a final mocking grin before disappearing once more.

"What are we going to do, Liz?" Jessica said miserably. "How are we going to get back to Cornwall?"

"Oh, we'll think of something," said Lizzie. "We'll *have* to. Now then, where did you put the cat?"

"The cat? Well, I think I put it in my drawer," Jessica said slowly.

"You *think*? Aren't you sure?"

"Yes – er – I mean no. I haven't seen it for ages."

"Come on, let's go and look," Lizzie said briskly.

But the cat wasn't in Jessica's dressing-table drawer. It wasn't anywhere in her room. Or in Lizzie's room either.

"When did you have it last?" Lizzie asked. "Come on, Jess, think. It's important."

"I know it's important," Jessica wailed. "I can't remember!"

"Perhaps it's downstairs," Lizzie suggested. "In the front room perhaps."

But the cat wasn't in the front room. Or the kitchen. Or anywhere in the house for that matter. It looked as though the black china cat had vanished completely.

Chapter 7

Jessica and Lizzie spent the rest of that day searching for the china cat. They looked under beds, inside drawers and behind cupboards until, in the end, they had to admit defeat. The cat had disappeared and with it their only chance of getting Beryl back to Cornwall. Of the ghost herself there was no sign, but Jessica guessed that she was watching their every move and might appear at any moment to carry out some terrible revenge.

"What are we going to do?" Jessica asked as she emerged hot and dusty from searching the garden shed. It was the last place where one would expect the ornament to be but they felt they had to look everywhere. "We'll never get Beryl back to the cottage now."

"There's nothing else for it," Lizzie said. "We'll have to ask Mum if she's seen it."

"But she'll be furious," Jessica said. "I promised to send the cat back to Mrs Pengelly with a letter of apology."

Lizzie shrugged. "Can't be helped," she said.

As Jessica had predicted, their mother was very angry indeed when they asked her. "No, I haven't seen that cat," she fumed. "I'd assumed you'd already sent it back to Mrs Pengelly as I asked."

"I was going to," Jessica said feebly. "I just hadn't quite got round to it yet."

"Why not? You've had plenty of time. I don't know what's got into you these days, Jessica. You always used to be such a quiet, responsible girl. But now—"

"I've had things to do," Jessica said sullenly. "And I *was* going to send the cat back, I really was."

Her mother sighed. "Well, just make sure

you find it. And I want to see your letter to Mrs Pengelly before you send it off. That cat is her property, not ours, and if it's lost or broken we'll have to replace it or pay for it. Correction. *You'll* have to replace it or pay for it. Understand?"

Jessica nodded. "So you haven't seen it any–where? Are you quite sure?"

"I've already told you," her mother said firmly. "No, I haven't. Have you asked Andrew?"

They found Andrew in the front garden, mowing the lawn. He was glad of an excuse to stop.

"A black china cat," he said thoughtfully. "Yes, I did see it somewhere."

Jessica and Lizzie exchanged excited glances. "You did? Where? What's happened to it?"

"Hang on, I'm trying to remember," Andrew said. "Let's see now. It was a couple of days ago. Oh yes, I found it lying on the living room floor. It was a bit chipped and I didn't think it was worth keeping so I put it in the bag with the other things to go to the next jumble sale."

"Which bag?" Jessica demanded. "Where is it? We need to find it."

"In the cupboard under the stairs," he said. "But what's the hurry? Why are you so keen to find that cat? It was just a cheap ornament, not worth anything."

"It wasn't ours," Lizzie explained. "We brought it back from Cornwall by mistake. We've got to send it back to Mrs Pengelly."

"Does it really matter?" Andrew asked. "I'm sure Mrs Pengelly hasn't missed it. And even if she has I don't expect she'd mind you keeping it if that's what you—"

"Oh, you don't understand," Lizzie said impatiently. "We've got to send it back. It's *important*."

Andrew shrugged and switched on the mower again. "Can't see what all the fuss is about," he said. But the girls didn't hear him – they were already halfway back to the house.

Lizzie reached the hall cupboard first and

flung open the door. She peered inside at the collection of odd cardboard boxes and ancient wellies and then turned to Lizzie. "It's not here," she said. "The bag's not here."

"It must be," Jessica said impatiently. "Let me look."

But there was no bag of jumble in the cupboard.

"It must be somewhere else," Jessica said. "Ask Mum."

"Do we have to?" Lizzie asked. "She'll only yell at us again."

"Of course we have to," Jessica said. "Unless, of course, you actually *want* Beryl to stay with us for ever."

"No, of course I don't," Lizzie said. "Let's find Mum. *I'll* ask her."

They turned to go in search of their mother but just then Andrew came in through the front door and said, "I've just remembered something."

"We can't find the bag," Jessica said accusingly.

"That's what I've just remembered,"

Andrew said. "Someone came to the door the day before yesterday and asked if we had any jumble for her charity shop. And so I gave her the bag."

"With the cat inside it," Jessica said dully.

"With the cat inside it," Andrew said. "Sorry about that. If I'd known it was important I wouldn't have put it in the bag in the first place."

"You weren't to know," Jessica said generously, trying to look more cheerful than she felt. "It's not your fault."

Andrew turned to go but stopped when Lizzie said, "Which charity shop was it?"

"Why do you want to know?" Jessica asked. "It's gone and that's all there is to it."

"No, it isn't," Lizzie said. "If we know which shop it was, then we can go and get the cat back. We can even buy it from them, if we have to."

"*Buy* it?" Jessica said scornfully. "You must be joking."

"We'll have to if that's the only way of getting the cat back." Lizzie turned back to

Andrew. "Can you remember which shop it was?"

"I can, as it happens," he said. "It was SOFF."

"Soff?" Jessica asked scornfully.

"That's right," said Andrew. "SOFF. Save Our Furry Friends. It's an animal rescue charity."

"I know the one," Lizzie said. "It's just across from the Oxfam shop. Thanks, Andrew."

He smiled and said, "Glad to be of help," before turning round and going back outside to the lawnmower.

"Come on, Jess, let's go," Lizzie said, heading for the door.

Lizzie was halfway down the garden path by the time Jessica caught up with her. "Where are you going, Liz?" she panted. "What are we going to do?"

"There's only one thing *to* do," Lizzie said grimly. "We've got to get to that charity shop and buy the cat before anyone else does." She stopped dead. "I haven't got any money with me," she said. "I'll have to go back."

"It's all right," Jessica said. "I've got some in my pocket. Not much," she added quickly.

"Well, we won't need much. They're not going to charge a lot for a stupid little black china cat like that, are they?"

"You never know," said Jessica.

The Save Our Furry Friends shop was empty, except for a red-haired woman behind the counter and an old lady miserably sorting through a heap of old cardigans. Jessica and Lizzie walked past the shelves of books and the racks of clothes to a table at the back where the oddments were displayed: ornaments and old plates and chipped cups, and strange objects that weren't so easily identified. There were a couple of chipped china dogs and a shapeless creature that might have been a cow but there were no cats at all. Certainly not a black china one.

"Oh, look," said Lizzie. "There's that sweet little vase with lavender on it that we brought back from Norfolk the year before last. I didn't know that Andrew had thrown that out too. I wonder if I should buy it back?"

"Forget about that," Jessica said. "It's the cat we're after. And it certainly isn't here."

"Can I help you?" called the woman behind the counter. She was looking at them suspiciously, obviously convinced that they were shoplifters on the prowl.

"We were looking for a cat," Lizzie said sweetly. "A little black china cat. We donated it to the shop by mistake, you see, and we really need to have it back. It's—"

"It's a valuable family heirloom," said Jessica. "Worth a fortune. If we don't get it back we'll be in the most awful trouble. We'll pay for it, of course."

The woman relaxed her guard a little. "I can't say I've noticed a black cat," she said. "You gave it to us recently, did you?"

"A couple of days ago," Lizzie said. "Someone came to our house and we gave them a bag of jumble. And the cat was in it."

The woman gave a sudden smile. "Oh yes, I remember now. A black china cat *did* come in the other day. Sweet little thing it was. I'm not surprised it went so quickly. Nearly bought it myself." She beamed at them.

"Do you mean that it's been sold?" Jessica asked.

"Yes, that's right, dear," said the red-haired woman. "Someone's already bought it. Sorry, but you're too late."

Chapter 8

Lizzie stared at the woman behind the counter in disbelief. "Are you quite sure?" she asked. "Are you quite sure that the cat's been sold?"

The woman frowned. "Of course I'm sure. I'm sorry, dear, but you're too late. That's all there is to it. Now, was there anything else you wanted?"

"No, thank you," Jessica said, tugging at Lizzie's sleeve. "We only wanted the cat." And then, when Lizzie refused to budge, "Come *on*, Lizzie."

Lizzie turned and followed Jessica towards the door just as an older woman came in and joined the red-haired woman at the counter. She was wearing a bright green sweatshirt with a picture of a spaniel and the letters SOFF.

"What are we going to do now?" Lizzie whispered.

"I don't know," Jessica said. "Let's stop and think. We'd better pretend to be looking at these books or that woman will get suspicious."

Lizzie bent down and rummaged among the old books near the door. "Well?" she demanded. "Have you got any bright ideas?"

Jessica shook her head. "Perhaps it would be best to forget all about it."

"What do you mean?" Lizzie said, turning the pages of a thick book with a picture of a schoolgirl on the cover.

"I think we should tell Mum the truth," Jessica explained. "We'll just have to tell her that the cat has gone and that we'll replace it somehow. Or pay for it."

"And be stuck with Beryl for the rest of our lives? You must be joking. Hey, this book looks rather good. It's called *The Jolliest Term on Record* and the girls in the pictures look just like Beryl. I wonder how much it is?"

Jessica snatched the book from Lizzie and pushed it angrily back on the shelf. "You're not listening to a word I'm saying," she snapped. "Perhaps you'd rather stay here and read instead?"

"Keep your hair on," Lizzie said. "I was only looking. Anyway, we've got to pretend to be interested in the books or else that woman at the counter will think we're up to no good." She caught sight of Jessica's angry expression and went on quickly, "We could try and find another black cat to replace it."

"That might take ages," Jessica said. "And anyway, I shouldn't think it'll be any help. Beryl can only travel with something from Mrs Pengelly's cottage, remember? So we can't make do with any old cat."

"There's only one thing for it, then. We'll have to try and get our cat back."

"But how?" Jessica asked.

Lizzie shrugged. "I don't know."

"Are you quite sure there's nothing else I can do to help?" The red-haired woman had left the counter and was now pretending to sort through a box of old magazines beside the bookshelves.

"Well, there is, sort of," Jessica said. "We simply have to get that cat back. So we were wondering if you could remember who bought it. Then we could go and ask for it back."

The woman looked sceptically at her for a moment and then gave a loud sarcastic laugh. "You must be joking!" she snorted. "How do you expect me to remember who bought it? We don't ask our customers for their names and addresses, you know."

"There's no need to be nasty," Lizzie said severely. "We were only asking. For all we know, a friend of yours might have bought it."

The woman looked embarrassed and gave a nervous cough. "Well, as it so happens, I wasn't even here when it was sold," she said. "I only work mornings. So I don't know who bought it. But I wouldn't tell you even if I knew. Which I don't."

"What cat is this, then?" asked the woman in the green sweatshirt. And then, when Jessica had explained what they wanted, she said, "Oh, I remember that cat. A sweet little black china cat, wasn't it? Ethel Spindle bought it yesterday afternoon. I remember it particularly because I know she collects model cats and she was really pleased to find that one. She said it reminded her of one of her own cats. Pleased as Punch with it she was."

"You sure?" the red-haired woman asked.

"Of course I'm sure," her friend said. "I've known Ethel Spindle for years. Mad about cats she is."

"Do you know where she lives?" Lizzie asked eagerly.

"Why do you want to know?"

"Well, we'd like to go and see her and ask if she would sell the cat back to us."

The woman pursed her lips and looked doubtful. "Well, I don't know about that. I can't give our customers' names and addresses to all and sundry, can I?"

"We're not all and sundry," Jessica said indignantly, and Lizzie added, "Oh, *please*. It's really important. That cat came to you by mistake. We *have* to try and get it back or else we'll be in the most awful trouble. It's a matter of life and death."

"Oh, very well then," the woman said. "Ethel only lives down the road. It'll be best if I take you there myself, though, just to be on the safe side." She turned to the red-haired woman. "You won't mind if I pop out for a minute or two, will you, Phyllis?"

Phyllis obviously *did* mind but she sniffed and said, "I suppose it's all right. But don't blame me if we get a rush of customers and I can't manage on my own."

The woman in the green sweatshirt took a look round the shop. It was completely empty, apart from the old lady sorting through cardigans. "I'm sure you'll cope, dear," she said acidly, and then turned to the girls. "Come on, you two. I'll show you where Ethel Spindle lives."

Jessica and Lizzie followed the woman out

of the shop and then down the hill towards
the tube station. After a while she turned
down a side street and then down another
before coming to a stop outside a small house.

"Here we are," she said, ringing the doorbell. "I'll just see if Ethel's in."

The girls stared at the house. It looked as
though it had seen better days: the front door
badly needed painting and the tiny front
garden was choked with nettles and weeds. A
large bad-tempered tabby cat was sitting on
top of an overflowing dustbin just inside the
gate. It hissed at Lizzie when she tried to
stroke it.

After a while the front door slowly opened
and an old lady peered out.

"Ah, there you are, Ethel," said the woman.
"I've brought you some visitors. They've a
favour to ask you."

The old lady opened the door wider and
Jessica and Lizzie went inside. The woman in
the green sweatshirt stayed where she was
and said, "Well, I'll love you and leave you,
Ethel dear. I've got to get back to the shop or

else there'll be hell to pay from that Phyllis."
She waved at the girls and walked briskly
back down the street.

The old lady ushered the girls into an untidy sitting room. There were cats everywhere: pictures of cats on the walls, model
cats on the mantelpiece, miniature china and
pottery cats in a glass-fronted cupboard.
There were real cats, too, perched on the sofa
and curled up in armchairs – a black long-
haired cat, two ginger ones and several tabbies.

"Now then," said the old lady. "What can I
do for you?"

Lizzie explained why they had come and
then Miss Spindle said, "Well, yes, I did buy
a black china cat from the Furry Friends shop
the other day. That one." She pointed at a
display cabinet in a corner and there, on the
top shelf, was the cat. *Their* cat.

"Yes, that's the one!" Lizzie said excitedly.
"Oh, how wonderful! Can we buy it back
from you?"

Miss Spindle looked at her thoughtfully.
"Well, I don't rightly know," she said slowly.

"Normally I'd tell you to go away and mind your own business. I bought that cat fair and square. It's my property now. But I'm not really sure about it. There's something about that cat…" She glanced at the ornament and then shivered and looked quickly away again.

"What do you mean?" Jessica asked, puzzled. "What sort of something?"

"I don't really know," the old lady said. "It's difficult to put into words. It's as if – as if that cat doesn't like being here. As if it belongs somewhere else. It – it doesn't fit in somehow. It's not happy." She smiled at the girls. "It sounds silly, I know, but I really think there's something evil about that cat. I wish I'd never brought it home."

"Then you won't mind if we buy it from you?" Jessica said eagerly.

"No, dear," Miss Spindle said wearily. "Take it back and welcome. But I don't want money for it. Just give a donation to the Furry Friends shop."

The old lady got to her feet and crossed to the cabinet. She opened the door and took out the black china cat and then handed it to Jessica.

"Thank you very much indeed," Jessica said. "We're really grateful, aren't we, Lizzie?"

Lizzie nodded eagerly, and then turned and led the way to Miss Spindle's front door. "Thank you very much," she called as they walked down the path to the gate.

"That's all right, dear," Miss Spindle said as she closed the door. "Good luck!"

As soon as they got home, the girls ran upstairs to Jessica's room and hid the cat carefully in her dressing-table drawer once more.

"Thank goodness that's over!" Jessica said, sprawling on her bed.

"I don't know what we'd have done if someone else had bought the cat," Lizzie said. "It was a real stroke of luck that Miss Spindle was a friend of the woman in the charity shop."

"I know," said Jessica. "But we don't have to worry any more. We've got it back now."

"So you've found it at last!" said Beryl.

Lizzie gasped, and Jessica jumped to her feet. The ghost was leaning casually against the doorpost, a triumphant leer on her thin face.

"Hello, you two," she said. "How ripping that you got the cat back. I don't know what I'd have done if you hadn't found it. I'd have been forced to stay here for ever, I suppose. And you wouldn't have liked that, would you?" Her dark eyes glittered spitefully behind her wire-framed glasses.

Jessica sat down on her bed again. "No, we wouldn't have liked that," she said. "But *you* wouldn't have liked it either, would you?"

Beryl gave her a thoughtful stare. "No, I wouldn't," she said. "I want to go back home. I want to go back to the cottage. In Cornwall."

"All right, then," Jessica said calmly. "We'll take you back."

"And about time too. I've been waiting long enough."

"But we'll only take you back on one condition," Jessica went on.

Beryl looked at her suspiciously. "Go on."

"There must be no more haunting until we

go," Jessica said. "No haunting at all. No noises, no screaming, no scary laughter. No throwing things, no tripping people up, no rude notices on the bulletin board. We want to forget that you're here at all."

"And what if I don't agree?" Beryl asked sullenly.

"If you don't agree, then we'll never take you back. You'll be stuck here for ever."

Beryl stared doubtfully at Jessica. It was obvious that she wasn't sure whether to believe her or not.

"You're going to be as quiet as a mouse," Jessica went on. "If there's the slightest peep out of you then we'll never take you back to Cornwall. You'll never go home again. Do you understand?"

Beryl glared at her, her eyes cold and dark and vindictive.

"I understand," she muttered. "But it's not fair. How can I possibly—"

"It's entirely up to you," Jessica said. "Either you keep quiet and go back home as soon as we can arrange it, or else you carry on as usual and stay here for ever and ever. The choice is yours."

Beryl said nothing but continued to stare at Jessica. Then, at last, she said, "All right, then. I promise."

Jessica gazed at her in triumph. "Do you really mean it? Do you really promise?"

"Yes," said Beryl sullenly. "I mean it. I promise. I *promise*!"

She gave the girls a final defiant glare and then faded away as quickly as she had appeared.

Chapter 9

Beryl was as good as her word. They saw nothing of her at all during the next few days and there were moments when Jessica began to feel that she must have been imagining everything that had happened. Life now seemed so normal and ordinary and *dull* that she even began to miss having Beryl around. But, as Lizzie reminded her, you could never be quite sure what might happen next.

"There's no knowing what she might do if she gets bored," Lizzie pointed out. "She was nice for a while at the cottage, remember? She used to play Monopoly with us and watch *Neighbours*. But that soon stopped when she got bored."

"You're right," Jessica said gloomily. "I'd forgotten all about that. And we must always remember that she could pop up at any time."

It was strange to think that Beryl was always there, just out of sight, listening, watching, waiting to pounce. They might not be able to see her but that didn't mean that the house wasn't haunted any more. And then, as if to prove it, Jessica woke up one morning to find Beryl perched on the end of her bed, looking impatient.

"What are you doing here?" Jessica asked. "I thought you promised to keep out of the way until we get you back to Cornwall."

"I'm not doing anything," Beryl said. "I'm just sitting here. What's wrong with that?"

"I don't trust you," Jessica said. "But I still mean it, you know. Any more of your tricks and it's bye-bye Cornwall."

"I haven't forgotten," Beryl said complacently. "I just thought I'd put in an appearance to remind you."

"To remind me of what?"

"To remind you of *your* side of the bargain," Beryl said. "I haven't noticed any suitcases being packed. I haven't heard anyone talking about what to wear on the beach and how many jigsaw puzzles to take in case it rains." She paused and gave Jessica a thoughtful stare. "I do hope you haven't forgotten about our little trip to Cornwall. I really do hope so."

"No, I haven't forgotten," Jessica said. "You don't think I want you hanging around here for ever, do you? We have to take things slowly, that's all. We've got to show my mother and Andrew that we're behaving ourselves. I'll speak to them soon, I promise."

"Well, just see that you do," Beryl said sweetly. "Otherwise I might just have to throw a few plates about to remind you that I'm waiting."

"No, please," Jessica said quickly. "I *will* speak to them. But I've got to pick the right moment."

The right moment arrived sooner than any of them had expected. As she was clearing the table after lunch the next day, Jessica's mother smiled at her and Lizzie and said, "I'm so glad that you two have seen sense at last."

"What are you talking about?" Lizzie asked innocently, knowing full well what she meant.

"You're behaving yourselves again," their mother said. "You've stopped all that banging about and throwing things and fighting. I feel as though I've got two daughters again instead of two raging lunatics."

Jessica smiled at her and then said carelessly, "Wouldn't it be wonderful if we were on holiday again? It was such a pity that we had to leave the cottage before our time was up."

"Well, whose fault was that?" said Andrew. "If it hadn't been for what you did—"

"Yes, I know," Jessica said quickly. "But we're different now. We'd never behave like that again."

"She's right, you know," her mother said. "It *was* a shame that we had to cut short the holiday. I feel a bit cheated, really. It's as if we're still owed a few more days away."

84

"It was so lovely at Ottercombe," Lizzie said. "The beach and the cliffs and the walks—"

"And having to explain to Mrs Pengelly why we made such a mess of her cottage," Andrew interrupted.

"She knows we didn't mean it," Jessica said. "She knows that we're a well-behaved family really."

"It's half-term next week," Lizzie said. "Couldn't we go away again? Just for a couple of days?"

Jessica's mother smiled at Andrew and put her hand on his. "It *would* be nice, wouldn't it?"

"We'd be really good this time," Jessica said. "Nothing will go wrong, I promise you."

Andrew sat back in his chair and stared at the others. "I don't believe I'm hearing this," he said slowly. "We're not made of money, you know. How can we afford to go away again? And anyway, the weather will be terrible down there at this time of year."

"Nonsense!" said Jessica's mother. "Cornwall's beautiful in October, and we'll have the beaches to ourselves. It's out of season, remember. All the holidaymakers will have gone home."

"But—" Andrew began, but she took no notice.

"We can afford a couple of days away," she went on. "It'll be much cheaper, anyway, because it's out of season."

"Oh, *please*!" said Jessica, and Lizzie added, "We must go, we *must*!"

Andrew was silent for a moment or two and then a smile spread slowly across his face. "I can see I'm outnumbered," he said. "OK, we'll go to Ottercombe for a couple of days at half-term. If I can get time off work, that is. And if we can find somewhere to stay."

"Go and phone now," Jessica said. "Go and phone Mrs Pengelly now."

"Go and phone *Mrs Pengelly*?" said Andrew in surprise. "You must be joking!"

"No, I'm not," said Jessica. "It'd be really nice to go back to the cottage we were at before. Mrs Pengelly's cottage. We really liked it there."

"Oh, yes, please," said Lizzie. "It wouldn't be the same anywhere else. It must be the cottage. It *must*!"

Andrew gave the girls a puzzled look, and their mother said, "But we can't go back there."

"Why not?" asked Jessica.

"Do you honestly think that Mrs Pengelly would have us back after what happened last time? She had to have the cottage redecorated, remember?"

"But—" Lizzie began.

"No buts about it," her mother said firmly. "And anyway, even if she *did* agree to have us back, I wouldn't be able to look her in the face again after what happened. No, it'll have to be somewhere else. We're not going back to Mrs Pengelly's cottage and that's all there is to it."

There was silence for a moment or two. Jessica swallowed hard, trying to hide her disappointment. Oh well. They'd have to think of some other way of getting Beryl back. The main thing was to keep the news from her. If she found out, then anything might—

There was a sudden crash behind her. She turned round and saw that the bulletin board had fallen from the wall and postcards and cuttings and slips of paper were scattered across the floor.

Andrew got to his feet and started to pick them up. "How very odd," he said. "I can't think how that could have happened. I could have sworn this board was securely fixed."

Jessica said nothing. She sat at the table, numb with misery. She knew exactly how it could have happened. Beryl had heard that they couldn't go back to the cottage and had lost her temper. There'd be even worse to come now. None of them would get a wink of sleep that night. She'd make their lives a misery, and there'd be no end to it. Beryl would haunt their house for ever.

Andrew started to fix the bulletin board back on the wall. "It isn't quite as bad as all that, you know," he said. "Mrs Pengelly's cottage isn't the only one in Ottercombe. There are plenty of others. I'll see if I can find somewhere else for us to stay."

"But it won't be the same!" Lizzie wailed. "I want to go back to the same cottage."

"Does it matter?" asked her mother, puzzled. "We'll still be in Ottercombe. We'll be very near the other cottage. You could go and look at it if you feel so strongly about it."

"Could we?" Lizzie said, her eyes shining. She turned to Jessica. "We could go and look at the other cottage, Jess! That'll be better than nothing, won't it?"

"I wish I knew why that cottage was so important to you," her mother said with a worried look on her face.

"It was just that we liked it there so much," Jessica said quickly. Then, raising her voice, she went on, "But I'm sure that another cottage will be just as nice. Nicer even. And, as Lizzie says, we'll be able to go and look at the first cottage whenever we want."

"There's no need to shout," Andrew said with a frown. "Anyone would think you were trying to tell the neighbours."

Jessica smiled. No, not the neighbours, she

thought to herself. Just Beryl. She just wanted Beryl to know that they would be able to take her home after all.

Chapter 10

"It seems really strange to be back here again," Lizzie said.

Jessica stretched out on a rock and stared up at the sky. It was a pale watery blue, apart from some threatening clouds. If she shut her eyes and forgot about the wind tugging at her hair and the chill breeze nipping her fingers, she could pretend she was on one of those romantic Caribbean beaches that they show on television travel programmes.

"It feels as though it was years ago when we were here before," Lizzie went on.

Jessica sat up and scowled at her. It wasn't easy to imagine that you were lying on a romantic beach when there was a diseased swamp monster called Lizzie sitting beside you, talking her head off.

She looked round for Beryl. She was paddling aimlessly at the sea's edge, and Jessica smiled to herself. Beryl looked really odd and out of place there. She had tucked her creased gym-slip into her knickers but she hadn't bothered to take off her thick blue stockings. Mind you, they didn't seem to be getting wet, so perhaps it didn't matter. Perhaps ghosts weren't affected by water. Then how did they wash? Perhaps they didn't. Perhaps you didn't need to keep clean if you were a ghost. Perhaps you were clean all the time. She must remember to ask Beryl about that.

There was no one else on the beach, apart from a family on the far side, a man and woman with a pretty fair-haired girl of about twelve who was presumably their daughter. She kept giving Beryl curious glances, and who could blame her.

"I can't get used to Beryl behaving herself for a change," Lizzie said.

Jessica had to agree that the change in Beryl's behaviour had been remarkable. As soon as it had been decided that they were going back to Cornwall together, there hadn't been a peep out of her. They had *seen* quite a bit of her, though. Sometimes, when the adults were out of the way, she would appear without warning and join in with whatever Jessica and Lizzie were doing. They came to enjoy her unexpected appearances, and it was exciting to know that a ghost might suddenly appear to join them in a game of Scrabble or just sit and watch television with them. It was strange to think that this ghostly girl with her old-fashioned hairstyle and weird school uniform would have been an old lady in her seventies if she hadn't been knocked off her bicycle all those years ago.

Beryl had behaved herself on the journey to Cornwall too. Jessica had wrapped the china cat very carefully in a towel and packed it at the bottom of her suitcase. And, as long as Jessica or Lizzie remembered to bring the cat with them, Beryl was able to come down to the beach. True, Beryl didn't think much of the cottage they were staying in, but, apart from some bad-tempered muttering in Jessica's ear, she had so far kept her dissatisfaction to herself. The others liked the new cottage; it was on the opposite side of the cove from Beryl's old home but they had a good view of it from the garden.

"We've got to decide how to get the cat back to Mrs Pengelly's cottage," Jessica said.

"Why don't we break in at dead of night?" Lizzie suggested.

"Oh, very clever, I must say," Jessica sneered. "What if someone sees us? How are you going to explain it to the police? Please, officer, we didn't come here to steal anything, we came to put something back."

Lizzie went red. "It was only an idea," she mumbled.

"And not a very good one," Jessica snapped.

"Well, *you* think of something better then, if you're so clever."

There was a pause, and then Jessica said, "*I* think we should try and find out if anyone's staying in Mrs Pengelly's cottage. And if there *are* people there, we should get really friendly with them. Then they might invite us to the cottage for tea, and we could take the cat with us and leave it there."

"But what if they find the cat after we've gone and return it to us?" Lizzie asked.

"We'd have to hide it somewhere," Jessica said. "Where they couldn't find it."

"Well, I think you're making it all too complicated," Lizzie said. "I think we should go to Mrs Pengelly and tell her the truth."

"The truth?" Jessica said aghast. "You must be joking."

"Not the complete truth," Lizzie said irritably. "I don't mean we should tell her about Beryl. I think we should just tell her that we took the cat away by mistake and that we'd like to return it."

Jessica thought about this. "I suppose we *could* do that," she said slowly. "But we couldn't be sure that Mrs Pengelly would take it straight back to the holiday cottage. She might decide to keep it in her own home.

No, I think my idea's worth a try. We've got to get to know the people who are staying in the cottage. And then get the cat inside somehow."

"And how do you propose we get to know them?" Lizzie wanted to know. "Go and knock on the door and say, 'Hello, we want to get to know you and can we come inside your house, please?'"

"We can ask Mrs Pengelly," Jessica said. "We can go and see her and say we want to meet the people in the cottage. And then she'll take us there and introduce us."

"Yes, it might work, I suppose," Lizzie said. "The main thing is to get the cat back inside the cottage, come what may. Beryl's sure to get bored with being good before long, and the last thing we want is her getting up to her old tricks in this new cottage. Where is she, anyway?"

Jessica stood up. "Still paddling. Let's go and join her. Come on." She set off towards the water's edge.

"It's odd, isn't it?" Lizzie said thoughtfully.
"What is?"

"Beryl on the beach. You only think of ghosts in old castles and ruined abbeys and graveyards. You don't think of them by the sea. And you only think of them as horrid shapes or headless skeletons, not as ordinary girls like us."

"Beryl's not ordinary," Jessica said. "And she's not like us."

"No, but she isn't a headless skeleton either," Lizzie pointed out.

There was really no answer to that, and so they walked on towards the water. They paddled for a while and then wandered along the beach, collecting shells and unusual pebbles as they went, and searching for anything interesting that might have been washed up by the tide. It was Jessica's ambition to find a message in a bottle but she hadn't had any luck so far.

It wasn't long before they drew level with the other family. The parents were sitting on the sand, reading newspapers, but the girl was paddling in the shallows. She looked up when they approached and Jessica gave her a friendly smile but she didn't respond. She just gave them a sulky stare. Jessica shrugged and turned back to Lizzie.

Afterwards, no one could remember who started the splashing, but Jessica was certain that it was Beryl. It was just the sort of thing she would do, especially if she was beginning to get bored. At the time, though, all Jessica knew was that she was suddenly soaking wet because someone had splashed her.

With a roar she launched herself at Lizzie, who mounted a vigorous counterattack. The air was filled with sand and spray and the sound of laughter. Someone sent water splashing into Jessica's eyes and she stumbled and fell against Lizzie. She lost her balance too, and landed flat on her back in the sea. With an angry yell she leaped to her feet and soon they were both pushing and struggling and falling.

And then, suddenly, they heard a scream that they didn't recognize and Jessica stopped to see the fair-haired girl lying in the water. "Sorry," Jessica panted, although she didn't know whether it was she who had knocked the girl over or someone else. The girl tried to get up but at the same moment Lizzie gave Jessica a hefty shove and she fell heavily against the girl and knocked her down again, this time flat on her face. She screamed again, much louder this time.

The others stopped fighting then and watched in silence as the girl struggled to her feet. Then there was the sound of an angry voice behind them, and they turned round.

"What on earth do you hooligans think you're doing?" It was the girl's father. He was standing at the sea's edge, waving a newspaper at them. "Leave her alone! Leave my daughter alone!"

"We weren't doing anything," Jessica said, and Lizzie added, "It was an accident. She got in the way, that's all."

"Don't give me that," the man said nastily. "I saw what happened. You picked on her. You're nothing but a couple of bullies. You should be banned from beaches like this, you should." He plodded into the water and took the girl by the hand. "Come on, Delphine. We'll find somewhere quieter."

Jessica and Lizzie watched in silence as the two of them staggered up the beach together. "You should be ashamed of yourselves," the man shouted back at them. "Pick on someone your own size next time."

Jessica could stand it no longer. "She's twice the size of both of us put together!" she yelled back. "She should look where she's going in future!"

The man stopped and turned. For a moment it looked as if he was about to come back again but he changed his mind and staggered on up the beach.

"What a pain in the neck," Jessica muttered. "We didn't do anything. It was an accident. She just got in the way."

"Of course she did," said Lizzie. "She should have looked where she was going."

"She should have looked where *we* were going," Jessica said, and laughed. "Anyway, that fight was good while it lasted. It's a pity that darling Delphine didn't join in like any normal human being would have done. Come on, we'd better be going. We said we'd be back by six."

She grinned at Lizzie and then noticed for the first time that Beryl had disappeared. Then she shrugged and thought no more of it. The ghost had probably made herself scarce because she didn't want to be seen by Delphine and her father. But she'd soon be back. They could be sure of that.

It was soon after breakfast the next morning that Jessica and Lizzie set off to visit Mrs Pengelly. She lived in a neat modern bungalow right next door to the cottage that had been Beryl's childhood home and where they had all stayed on their first visit to Ottercombe.

Mrs Pengelly was hanging out washing when they arrived at her house and her jaw dropped when she saw the girls.

"Goodness me, fancy seeing you two again," she said suspiciously. "Down here on a visit, are you?"

"Just for a couple of days," Jessica said.

"We're staying on the other side of the cove."

"In a cottage?" Mrs Pengelly asked.

Jessica nodded. Mrs Pengelly didn't say anything but Jessica could tell that she was dying to know whether the new cottage was still in one piece.

"We fancied a change of scene," Lizzie said.

"Just as well," Mrs Pengelly muttered.

It was then that Jessica told her about the black china cat, and how they'd taken it away with them by mistake. "We'd like to put it back in the cottage," she said. She stuck her hand in her pocket to make sure that the cat was still safe, and wondered whether to give it back to Mrs Pengelly now.

"Oh, there's no need to go to all that trouble," Mrs Pengelly said. "Just give it to me and I'll put it somewhere suitable. It might look rather nice in my spare room, now I come to think of it."

This was just what they had been afraid of. Jessica quickly took her hand out of her pocket and said, "I'm afraid I forgot to bring the cat with me. It's still at the other cottage.

But we'd really like to put it back ourselves, if you don't mind. In the place where it came from. We'd really like to do that."

Mrs Pengelly stared at her suspiciously for a moment. "Well, there are people staying in the cottage at the moment so you can't just barge in. Tell you what, though, we can pop round now, if you like, and see if they're at home. If I introduce you then you can arrange with them when to bring the cat back. Mr and Mrs Withers are such a nice couple. And they've got a lovely daughter about your age. I'm sure she'll be pleased to meet you. She'll be glad of some young company while she's here."

Jessica gave Lizzie a triumphant grin as they followed Mrs Pengelly to the cottage next door. It really looked as though the end was in sight at last. They would soon be saying goodbye to Beryl for ever.

Mrs Pengelly rang the doorbell and then turned to Jessica. "It must seem strange being back again," she said.

Jessica smiled at her. "Yes, it does."

The door opened then, and a girl appeared.

"Hello, dear," Mrs Pengelly said. "I've brought some people to meet you."

The girl stared at Jessica and the others with a face like thunder. "We've already met," she said.

Jessica stared back at the girl and her heart sank. Yes, they *had* already met.

It was Delphine.

There was no hope now of ever getting back inside the cottage.

Chapter 11

"So you've already met?" Mrs Pengelly said. "Well, that's a coincidence! Then you won't need any introductions from me, will you?"

Jessica shook her head numbly. She could hardly believe their bad luck. They had been so close to getting Beryl back where she belonged and now it looked as though they'd never manage it.

Delphine stared grimly at Jessica and Lizzie. "Yes, we've met all right," she said.

Mrs Pengelly gave her a puzzled frown and then said briskly, "Well, I'll leave you all to get acquainted then. I've got a lot to do this morning. Oh, Jessica here has a favour to ask you, dear." She bustled busily away.

"What sort of favour?" Delphine said.

"Er – nothing," Jessica stammered. "I – I've changed my mind." There didn't seem to be any point in asking whether they could go inside the cottage. She knew exactly what the response would be.

Delphine shrugged and turned to go. She was just about to close the door when Lizzie said suddenly, "We've come to apologize."

Delphine stopped and turned back. Jessica stared at Lizzie in amazement but she took no notice. "We've come to apologize for knocking you over on the beach yesterday," Lizzie went on. "We didn't do it on purpose. I hope we didn't hurt you."

Delphine looked at her suspiciously. "Well, you did, as a matter a fact," she said. "My arm's still quite sore this morning."

"Oh dear," Lizzie said. "Poor you. Anyway, we just thought we'd better come to say we're sorry."

Delphine frowned. She clearly wasn't sure

whether Lizzie was joking or not. Then, having decided that Lizzie was being serious, she said, "That's all right. I shouldn't have got in the way, I suppose. I could see you coming."

Jessica looked angrily at Lizzie. "Now just a minute!" she began. "That isn't—"

"I hope your arm gets better soon," Lizzie said quickly, taking no notice of her sister. "And I hope we can be friends from now on."

Delphine seemed doubtful. "Well, I don't know about that," she said. "It all depends…"

There was the sound of footsteps behind her and then Delphine's father appeared in the doorway.

"What are you two doing here?" he demanded. "Come to make trouble here as well, have you? Well, we'll soon see about *that*!"

"No, it's all right, Dad," Delphine said. "They've come to apologize."

"Oh." Mr Withers clearly hadn't expected this. He gave them a hard stare and then said, "Well, I should think so too. Now go away and leave Delphine alone. We don't want to see either of you again."

He pulled Delphine inside the cottage and closed the door very firmly in their faces.

Jessica and her sister stared at the door for a moment or two in astonishment, and then they turned and began to make their way down the path to the gate. When they were out of sight of the cottage, they stopped and Jessica turned angrily on Lizzie.

"What on earth did you think you were playing at?" she demanded. "Apologizing to that potato head? We didn't go there to apologize. We wanted to get inside the cottage and leave the china cat there."

"I know *that*," Lizzie said scornfully. "Why do you think I apologized? You don't think I *meant* it, do you?"

"Well, why did you do it then?"

Lizzie sighed impatiently. "I can't believe you're so stupid. We have to get inside the cottage, don't we? But the only way we can do it is by being friendly with that awful girl and her slimeball parents. And the only hope we've got of being friendly with them is by apologizing."

Jessica gazed at her sister admiringly. "You can be quite clever sometimes, Liz," she said. "Why didn't I think of that?"

"Because you do things without thinking, that's why. Come on, let's go to the beach." Lizzie set off along the rocky path that curved down towards the sea, and Jessica trailed slowly behind her.

They spent the rest of the morning pottering about on the beach, exploring the caves and rock pools or else simply messing about in the sea. It was when they were on their way back up to the cottage for lunch that they saw Delphine coming down the path towards them.

Jessica stopped when she saw her, wondering whether to be friendly or not. In the end she didn't have to decide because Delphine gave her a smile and said, "I'm glad I've found you."

Jessica gaped at her. "Glad? I thought you hated the sight of us. Well, your dad does, anyway."

Delphine shrugged. "Oh, don't take any

notice of him. Anyway, he sent me to apologize to you."

Lizzie couldn't believe her ears. "Apologize to *us*?"

"Yes. He's sorry he was so nasty to you just now. And on the beach yesterday. He said things that he shouldn't have done."

The others looked at each other. "Well, that's OK," Jessica said awkwardly. "We really didn't mean any harm."

"He realizes that now," Delphine said. "That's why he wants to say sorry. Mum does too. So would you like to come up to the cottage for tea this afternoon? If you're not doing anything else, that is."

"No, we're not doing anything," Jessica said. "Not that I know of."

"Didn't Andrew say something about going to the seal sanctuary this afternoon?" Lizzie asked.

Jessica gave her a warning shove. "I don't think so," she said quickly. "We'd love to come to tea, Delphine. Thanks very much."

"Good," said Delphine. "Come at about

four o'clock. Bring that other girl with you, if you like."

Jessica and Lizzie looked at each other. "Which other girl?" they asked.

Delphine looked puzzled. "The girl who was with you yesterday. The one with the glasses and the funny blue stockings."

"Oh yes, her," Jessica said, with a nervous laugh. "We don't really know who she was — er — is. She was just tagging along. We'd never seen her before."

"Oh, well, never mind," said Delphine. "Just the two of you then. See you later." She gave them a bright smile and then turned and ran back up the path.

Lizzie waited until she was out of sight then turned to Jessica. "But Andrew *did* say we were going to see the seals this afternoon," she protested.

"I know," Jessica said impatiently. "But it's much more important to put the cat into the cottage. We can go and see the seals any time but this may be our only chance to get Beryl back where she belongs."

The next few hours seemed to drag by. Andrew had been surprised to hear of the last-minute invitation to tea with the Withers family but agreed to put off the trip to the seal sanctuary until the next day.

"You go off and enjoy yourselves," he said. "We'll be glad to have you out of our hair for a while."

"And make sure you behave!" Jessica's mother said. "Oh, by the way, Jess, did you return that cat to Mrs Pengelly?"

"Not yet," Jessica said. "But she knows I've got it. I'm taking it with me to the cottage today so I can put it back in its rightful place."

Their welcome at the cottage that afternoon was very different to their reception earlier in the day. Delphine flung open the door with a beaming smile and led them straight into the sitting room where her parents were waiting.

"Glad you could come," Mr Withers said. "Sorry about the misunderstanding and all that. I always fly off the handle."

"You can say that again!" his wife laughed. "He's always been quick tempered. Just take no notice – that's what I always do. Now, do sit down. Tea won't be long."

Jessica took a chair by the fireplace. The black china cat used to sit on the mantelpiece and, with any luck, she'd be able to put it back without anyone noticing. She felt in her pocket to make sure that the cat was still safe and then smiled politely at Delphine's mother who was talking about the weather.

"Mrs Pengelly tells me that you stayed here in the summer," Mr Withers said.

"Yes," said Jessica.

"She said you had to cut short your holiday," Mrs Withers said. "What a shame!"

"Yes, it was," said Jessica. "But there was – there was a sudden crisis. And we had to go back home."

"What a pity!" said Mrs Withers. "Still, you're back now. That's the main thing." It was obvious that she was dying to know what the crisis was and why they had returned so soon, but Jessica wasn't going to tell her.

There was an uncomfortable pause and then Mrs Withers said, "Why don't you take your friends into the garden, Delphine, while I see to the tea?" She bustled into the kitchen, and her husband followed her.

Delphine stood up. "Come on, then," she said. "Though I can't think why you should be interested in the garden. There's nothing to it. You could fit it into our bathroom at home three times over."

The others got to their feet and shuffled towards the door that led into the garden. Jessica hung back, easing the china cat out of her pocket. And then, when Lizzie and Delphine had disappeared outside, she placed the cat carefully on the mantelpiece. She took a step back and looked at it for a moment, hoping that Beryl was appreciating the importance of the occasion. But there was no sound from her and so, after giving the cat a final affectionate pat on its smooth china head, she followed the others outside.

It was while they were having tea that Mrs Withers noticed the cat. "I don't remember seeing that cat before," she said, putting down her plate. "That black china cat on the mantelpiece. I suppose it must have been there but I swear I haven't noticed it."

"Me neither," said Delphine, her mouth full of lemon cheesecake.

"Oh, it's always been there," Jessica said loudly. "I remember it well. Don't you, Lizzie?"

"Oh, yes," said Lizzie. "I noticed it particularly because I'm very fond of cats. It was definitely there when we stayed in the cottage."

"Oh, well, I expect you're right," Mrs Withers said, looking doubtful. "Still, I could have sworn it wasn't there this morning when I dusted. It's funny how the memory plays tricks, isn't it?"

"Hilarious," said Jessica, wondering why Delphine's mother wasted time dusting when she was on holiday. Her own mother didn't even bother much when they were at home. She always said there were better things to do with her time.

Suddenly a picture fell from the wall with a

loud crash.

They all turned to look at it in surprise, and Mr Withers said, "That gave me a fright. The hook must have worked loose. I'd better—"

And then Mrs Withers let out a screech as the cup of tea she was holding suddenly emptied itself in her lap. She jumped to her feet and said, "Oh dear, how clumsy of me." Then she let out another shrill scream as one by one plates and cups and saucers flew from the table and smashed against the walls.

"What on earth's going on?" Mr Withers shouted, and then Delphine let out a pitiful wail as a jug of orange squash rose slowly into the air and moved towards her. The others watched in fascinated horror as the jug slowly emptied over her head. Delphine burst into tears as the orange liquid cascaded over her hair and shoulders.

"It's you, isn't it?" Mr Withers shouted at Jessica and Lizzie. "It's you brats up to your tricks again. I knew you lot were no good the minute I set eyes on you. I'm going to—"

But they never found out what he was going

to do because a large chocolate sponge with layers of cream and a covering of thick chocolate icing flew through the air and landed right in his face, swiftly followed by a bowl of trifle.

"It's not us, it's not!" Jessica shouted, not knowing whether to laugh or cry.

"Of course it is!" Mrs Withers wailed. "It must be! Who else is there?" She fled shrieking into the kitchen, pursued by a plate of chocolate éclairs.

Then Jessica saw Beryl. She was standing at the far side of the room, laughing her head off. Jessica couldn't ever remember seeing her look so happy before. After a moment or two Beryl caught sight of Jessica and smiled at her. And then, when Jessica smiled back, the ghost gave her a wave. It was almost as if she was waving goodbye. Jessica waved back, and then Beryl slowly faded into a shimmering shape that hung in the air for a moment or two and then disappeared.

Jessica looked at the others, wondering whether anyone else had noticed. Mrs Withers was still shrieking in the kitchen and her husband was busily wiping cream and chocolate icing from his eyes. Delphine had her eyes tightly closed and was wailing at the top of her voice. They clearly hadn't seen anything. But she could tell from the delighted expression on her face that Lizzie had seen Beryl too.

Jessica smiled to herself and then stood up. "Come on," she said. "I think we'd better be going."

After all, there was nothing else for them to do. Beryl was home again at last.

Chapter 12

"I wish we didn't have to go home tomorrow," Lizzie said gloomily, staring out of the window. "It seems only yesterday that we arrived."

"Well, it was, almost," Jessica said.

"I know. The odd thing is that I feel quite sad at the thought of leaving. Last time I couldn't wait to get away. But now..."

"I know what you mean," Jessica said, joining her at the window and gazing out at the view of cliffs and cove and sea.

"And the oddest thing of all is that I'm really going to miss Beryl," Lizzie went on. "Stupid, isn't it? She's caused us nothing but trouble, and we've had a terrible time getting her back home. But I'm going to miss her."

Jessica nodded. She too found it hard to believe that they'd never again see that strange apparition in the creased black gym-slip and wrinkled blue stockings. They'd never see the pale thin face and the sharp black eyes behind the wire-rimmed spectacles or hear that familiar malicious laughter. Beryl had been such an important part of their lives that it was hard to imagine how they'd manage without her.

"Well, we could always go and visit Delphine," she said. "I'm sure Beryl would make an appearance if we went back."

"For old times' sake," Lizzie smiled. "No, I think she's best left where she is, don't you? In her old home. She's someone else's problem now. And I don't envy them." She paused, and then added, "Well, I don't *think* I do."

Jessica laughed. "I almost felt sorry for Mrs Withers after the tea party."

"Me too," Lizzie said. "But I think Beryl went too far that time. One or two smashed plates would have been enough. We'd have got the message."

"It was just her way of saying goodbye," Jessica said. "A sort of farewell performance."

There was a pause and then Lizzie said slowly, "I suppose she really *has* said goodbye?"

"What do you mean?" Jessica asked.

"Well, I wish I could be sure that Beryl really has gone."

Jessica gave a scornful laugh. "Of course she's gone," she said. "We took the cat back to the cottage. And you saw Beryl there with your own eyes. She's gone all right. We'll never see her again."

"But how can we be sure?" Lizzie said anxiously. "How can we be *really* sure?"

"I – I don't know," Jessica said. "But there's no need to worry, Liz. We've seen the last of Beryl, believe me. She'll never bother us again." She wished she felt as confident as she sounded so she decided to change the subject. "I'm going down to the beach. Coming?"

Lizzie shook her head. "It's my turn to

wash up the breakfast things," she said. "I'll come down and join you afterwards."

"See you later then," Jessica said.

It was still quite early and so the beach was almost deserted when Jessica arrived. This was the time she liked best. The tide had just gone out, leaving the sand clean and gleaming, and she was the only person there apart from a couple walking a dog in the distance and a girl wandering aimlessly at the water's edge.

It was only when she got closer that Jessica realized that the girl on the beach was Delphine. She stopped, wondering whether to go back or not, but then Delphine looked up and saw her.

"Hello," Jessica said nervously.

"Hello," said Delphine.

Jessica walked towards her. They'd seen nothing of Delphine or her parents since the terrible tea party and she was still feeling rather guilty. After all, if she hadn't taken Beryl back to the cottage then nothing unusual would have happened.

"I didn't think you'd still want to talk to me," Jessica said. "After all that happened."

"Well, it wasn't your fault, was it?" Delphine said.

Jessica stared at her. "Well, no. But I thought you might think it was. I thought you'd blame us."

Delphine looked puzzled. "But why should I blame you? It wasn't your fault that all those things happened." She came closer to Jessica. "If I tell you something, will you promise not to tell anyone else? Not even your sister?"

"Of course," said Jessica. She loved secrets, though she wasn't very good at keeping them.

"There was a note," Delphine said nervously. "There was a note on the bulletin board the morning after the – after you came to tea. My dad says that I must have written it because there was no one else who could have done it. But I didn't. I really didn't!"

"What sort of note?" Jessica asked.

Delphine took a crumpled piece of paper from the pocket of her jeans and handed it to Jessica. She unfolded it carefully and read:

Jessica smiled to herself. She now knew for certain that Beryl had returned to her old home and that they'd never see her again. She wasn't coming back. They were free at last. The haunting was over.

"Do you think it's true?" Delphine asked anxiously. "Do you think that the cottage really *is* haunted?"

Jessica looked at her. "Oh yes," she said. "It's haunted all right. But don't worry. She's a very friendly ghost." She started to walk away and then stopped to look back at Delphine. "Her name's Beryl, by the way. When you see her, tell her — tell her I said hello."

Then she walked on towards the rocks where Lizzie was waiting.